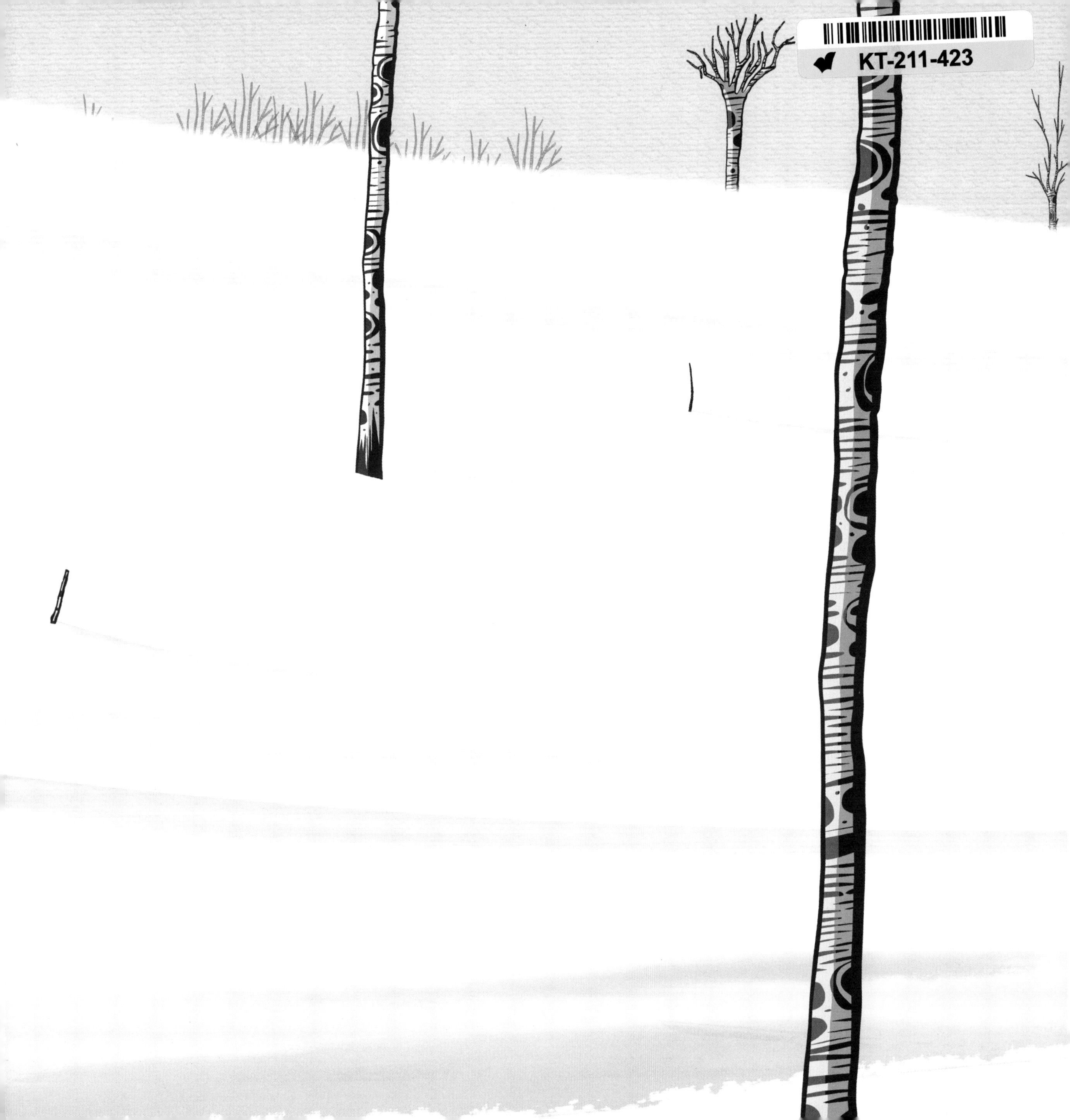

To Sam and Miriam with love, MZ
To Seán and Máire with love, AW

Rita Wants a Dragon published by Graffeg in 2022.
Copyright © Graffeg Limited 2022.

ISBN 9781914079665

First published by An tSnáthaid Mhór Teoranta 2018.

Text © Máire Zepf, illustrations © Andrew Whitson, design
and production Graffeg Limited. This publication and
content is protected by copyright © 2022.

Máire Zepf and Andrew Whitson are hereby identified as
the authors of this work in accordance with section 77 of the
Copyrights, Designs and Patents Act 1988.

A CIP Catalogue record for this book is available from the
British Library.

Mae Rita Eisiau Draig (Welsh edition) ISBN 9781914079948
Rita agus an Dragún (Irish edition) ISBN 9781912929191

The publisher acknowledges the financial support of the
Books Council of Wales. www.gwales.com

Teaching Resources
www.graffeg.com/pages/teachers-resources

1 2 3 4 5 6 7 8 9

GRAFFEG

This book belongs to

_____

_____

_____

_____

Rita

wants a Dragon

By Máire Zepf

Illustrated by Mr Ando

This is

Rita.

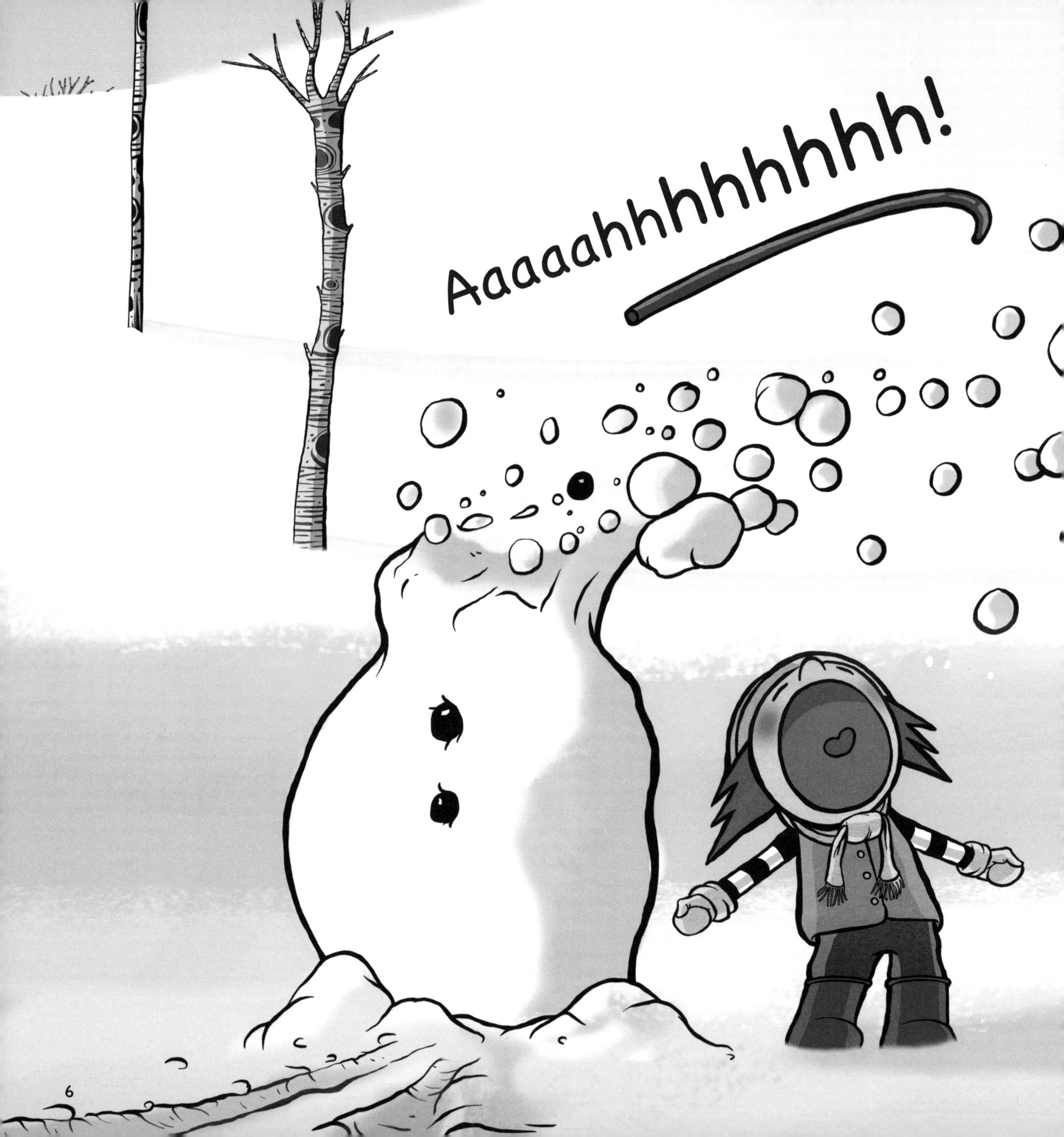
Aaaaahhhhhhhh!

Rita is cross.

Because **EVERYTHING** is wrong.

Rita wants a dragon.

Dragons are cross,
just like Rita.

Dragons roar,
louder than thunder.

Dragons breathe fire,
hot and angry.

Dragons stomp and thrash
and make the world shudder.

And when they are exhausted from roaring

and fire-breathing
and stomping,

they can fly...

far far away...

to somewhere quiet, all by themselves.

Rita would show her
dragon how to breathe,
slow and cool with no fire.

Her dragon wouldn't breathe flames anymore.

Or maybe just
a tiny bit.

They could talk about what had gone wrong.

They would cuddle up,
safe and warm

and live happily
ever after.

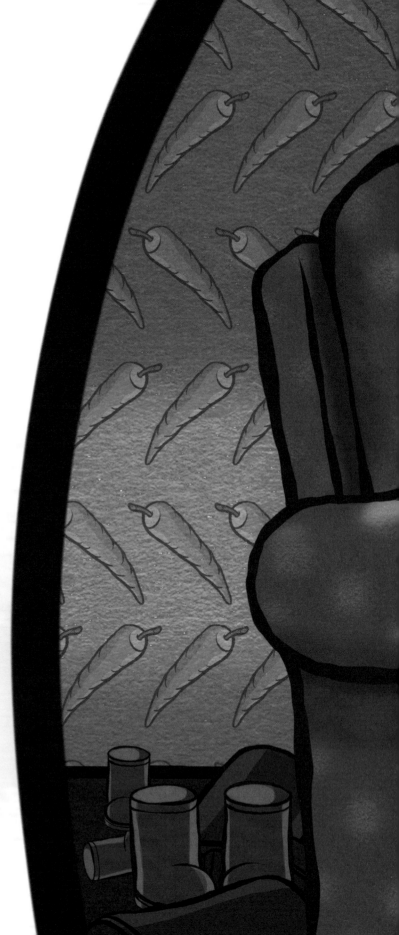